HERGÉ
★
THE ADVENTURES OF
TINTIN
★
CIGARS
OF THE
PHARAOH

EGMONT

The TINTIN books are published in the following languages:

Alsacien	CASTERMAN
Basque	ELKAR
Bengali	ANANDA
Bernese	EMMENTALER DRUCK
Breton	AN HERE
Catalan	CASTERMAN
Chinese	CASTERMAN/CHINA CHILDREN PUBLISHING
Corsican	CASTERMAN
Danish	CARLSEN
Dutch	CASTERMAN
English	EGMONT UK LTD/LITTLE, BROWN & CO.
Esperanto	ESPERANTIX/CASTERMAN
Finnish	OTAVA
French	CASTERMAN
Gallo	RUE DES SCRIBES
Gaumais	CASTERMAN
German	CARLSEN
Greek	CASTERMAN
Hebrew	MIZRAHI
Indonesian	INDIRA
Italian	CASTERMAN
Japanese	FUKUINKAN
Korean	CASTERMAN/SOL
Latin	ELI/CASTERMAN
Luxembourgeois	IMPRIMERIE SAINT-PAUL
Norwegian	EGMONT
Picard	CASTERMAN
Polish	CASTERMAN/MOTOPOL
Portuguese	CASTERMAN
Provençal	CASTERMAN
Romanche	LIGIA ROMONTSCHA
Russian	CASTERMAN
Serbo-Croatian	DECJE NOVINE
Spanish	CASTERMAN
Swedish	CARLSEN
Thai	CASTERMAN
Tibetan	CASTERMAN
Turkish	YAPI KREDI YAYINLARI

TRANSLATED BY
LESLIE LONSDALE-COOPER AND MICHAEL TURNER

EGMONT
We bring stories to life

Artwork copyright © 1955 by Editions Casterman, Paris and Tournai
Copyright © renewed 1983 by Casterman
Text copyright © 1971 by Egmont UK Limited
First published in Great Britain in 1971 by Methuen Children's Books
This edition published in 2012 by Egmont UK Limited,
The Yellow Building, 1 Nicholas Road, London, W11 4AN

Library of Congress Catalogue Card Numbers Afor 19681 and R 159731

Hardback: ISBN 978 1 4052 0803 1
Paperback: ISBN 978 1 4052 0615 0

CIGARS
OF THE
PHARAOH

This is the life, Snowy. A really quiet holiday for a change . . .

A holiday, indeed! I'd call it a deadly bore.

We'll be arriving in Port Said tomorrow. We go ashore for the day.

Then the Suez Canal, and Aden. We'll go ashore there, too.

I'd settle for Marlinspike.

Bombay, Colombo, then right on round, to finish in Shanghai.

How about that for a marvellous cruise, eh, Snowy?

Marvellous . . . You mean dull as ditchwater! . . . Why doesn't someone fall overboard to brighten things up?

Stop! . . . Stop! . . . HELP!

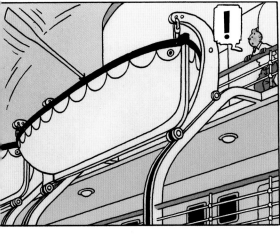

!

Excuse me, but what are you doing?

Surely you can see: I'm rowing.

But you're not in the water!

Nor I am! What an observant young man you are!

Now I wonder why I was rowing . . .

To rescue your papyrus, I expect. It blew overboard . . .

My papyrus? . . . My priceless manuscript? . . . Overboard? . . . Nonsense! I have it here.

But . . . I saw a paper blow into the sea!

What were we chasing, then?

Oh, yes . . . I remember now; it was just a travel brochure. You don't really think I'd let go of this do you? . . . My magnificent papyrus . . . the key to the lost tomb of the Pharaoh Kih-Oskh. Scores of Egyptologists have tried to find the spot . . .

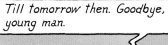

Every single one has vanished! But I, Sophocles Sarcophagus, shall be the first to reveal this wonder to the world.

I hope you will . . . But tell me, what's that queer symbol?

I don't know. I think it's the royal cipher of Kih-Oskh. But if you are interested, why not join me tomorrow in Port Said. We'll go on to Cairo, and find the place shown on my papyrus.

Good idea!

Till tomorrow then. Goodbye, young man.

What a strange fellow!

I beg your pardon, captain.

You clumsy nitwit! Can't you look where you're going?

So sorry, I mistook you for a ventilator . . .

Imbecile!

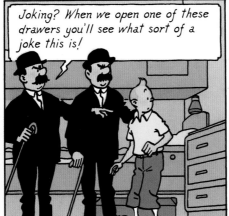
You? . . . Arrest me? You must be joking!

Joking? When we open one of these drawers you'll see what sort of a joke this is!

There! Someone tipped us the wink, and how right they were! Narcotics! That's heroin!

Next morning . . .

Who could have planted drugs in my cabin?

Someone who wanted me out of the way . . . But why?

Smells fishy!

Here we are in Port Said. Just a cable's length from the quay . . . and here I am, locked in the hold!

Hello . . . they're beginning to disembark . . . I wonder . . .

Come on, come on . . . drift a little bit closer . . .

I . . . er . . . could you possibly take us ashore?

A few minutes later . . .

Here we are, Snowy . . . in Port Said.

Well, well! What a pleasant surprise!

Happy New Year!

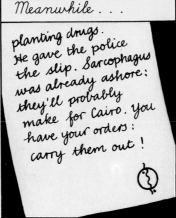
Meanwhile . . .

planting drugs. He gave the police the slip. Sarcophagus was already ashore: they'll probably make for Cairo. You have your orders: carry them out!

He won't get far, if my name's Thompson!

To be precise: if my name's Thomson we won't get far!

Later, somewhere near Cairo . . .

According to the papyrus the tomb can't be far away . . .

And soon . . .

You wait for us here. We will return this evening.

Yes, effendi!

You see, a discovery of this importance must be kept absolutely secret.

Yes, of course.

You seem to know the area very well.

I don't know it at all; the papyrus gives very detailed instructions.

We're getting very close now . . .

You have a remarkable sense of direction!

If the information is right, we shall find the tomb of Kih-Oskh at this very spot . . .

What did I tell you! The tomb! I've found it! O noble Pharaoh, I have come!

Fame at last! The name of Sophocles Sarcophagus will live for ever!

WOOAH WOOAH

Hello, what does Snowy want?

A cigar . . . A cigar out here . . . How peculiar.

Good heavens! That's extraordinary! The Pharaoh's emblem on the band!

FLOR
FINA

I wonder what Doctor Sarcophagus will make of that . . .

Hey! . . . What in the . . . ? He's gone!

I say, Tintin, it's just like the band of the cigar!

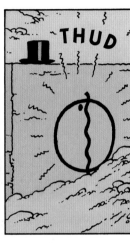

Fantastic! The Pharaoh's revenge! Here they are! The scholars who violated the tomb of Kih-Oskh . . . Poor devils, they paid dearly for their knowledge!

No! No! Never in a thousand years! No one's going to turn me into a mummy! We've got to get out of here, fast!

An umbrella! The Doctor's umbrella! Poor Sophocles Sarcophagus, what on earth's happened to him?

His shirt cuffs . . . and his tail coat . . . we've got to find him, Snowy!

Crumbs! Another door shutting us in!

Now we really are trapped by the Pharaoh . . . or one of his successors!

Hello . . . what's that over there?

Packing-cases . . . Let's have a look inside!

Great snakes! Full of cigars . . .

. . . all with that strange symbol!

Yes, they're absolutely identical with the one I picked up outside . . .

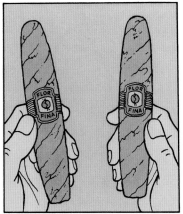

I wonder if the answer to all this lies hidden inside these cigars . . . I think I'd better take a look . . .

What . . . what's happening? . . . My head . . . I feel . . .

That smell . . . some sort of drug . . . someone's trying . . .

No! Not that!!

Meanwhile . . .

The bearded master told me to wait . . . When they did not return at nightfall I called loudly, I shouted . . . They did not answer me . . .

The next night . . .

Good. 'Sereno' is at the rendezvous. Unload the camels.

I'll flash the signal.

Ah, there's the caravan. Lower the boat right away.

Allah be with you, Mohammed . . . You've got the goods?

Yes, effendi. Everything is ready.

OK. And get a move on. The boss is worried about the coastguards . . .

Someone with a funny sense of humour, hiding the stuff in a coffin.

One of the boss's bright ideas, I expect.

Half an hour later . . .

That's the lot, skipper. All aboard.

Whew! Am I glad! Raise the anchor!

That's Allan's boat. We'll get him this time . . . the dirty smuggler!

Coastguards! Just my lousy luck! Sling the boxes overboard, fast!

SPLASH

An hour later . . .

Good thing we got rid of the evidence; they'd have nabbed me otherwise.

Message for you, skipper. It came while the cops were aboard.

Give it to me.

Three coffins shipped by mistake. They contain prisoners. Guard strictly pending fresh orders. Important. Repeat important.

That's torn it! They've been dumped! How can we find them now?

If there's nothing else to catch in this bit of sea we'll just have to starve to death . . .

. . . or else be drowned. The wind's rising and the sea's getting rough.

Ah, he's waking up at last!

Where am I?

Now I remember . . . We were hit by a gigantic wave . . . and that was that . . .

Hello, young Sinbad! How are you? . . . Slept well?

Yes, but how in the world did I get here?

Just happened to be passing, old boy, when you were going down for the third time!

You saved my life, Captain!

Forget it . . . But I must admit I'm dying to know what you were doing, floating around the Red Sea in a coffin.

I wish I knew that myself!

Ah, here's my passenger: Senhor Oliveira da Figueira, from Lisbon.

'Morning.

Delighted, dear sir, delighted!

Allow me to assist you, sir. Any little thing you may require, sir . . . and my prices will astonish you . . .

Just let me show you, sir. Absolutely no obligation. Now observe these exquisite ties . . .

Beautiful! . . . Beautiful! . . . Look how it suits you sir . . . matches your eyes . . . Quite, quite perfect . . .

And what about a sword? Real Toledo steel!

Everything a bargain! An alarm clock? A toothbrush? A biro?

Just as well I didn't fall for his patter. You end up with all sorts of useless junk if you're not careful.

That's the Arabian coast. We're landing there.

You can carry my things over there.

You're setting up shop? . . . Here? It's the middle of nowhere. You won't get a single customer!

Wait! I haven't started advertising yet.

Hello! Hello! Salaam Aleikum! Here we are again! Senhor Oliveira da Figueira at your service . . .

. . . bringing you the wonders of the western world. Walk up, my friends, walk up, don't be shy . . . don't miss this marvellous opportunity.

It's the solo supermarket!

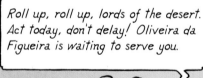

Roll up, roll up, lords of the desert. Act today, don't delay! Oliveira da Figueira is waiting to serve you.

What about this hat? Fit for a pharaoh! Make you the best-dressed man in the oasis!

This'll be a nice surprise for my wife!

There you are! Clean as a whistle. That's salesmanship for you! What's more, they all come back, too!

كـنـاك
! كـنـاك ؟

!

Son of a mangy dog! You sold me this cake! I ate it, and now look what's happened!

But . . . but that's a cake of soap!

Before the new moon rises, by Allah, my master Sheik Patrash Pasha will have you flogged!

Next morning . . .

Let's explore, Snowy . . .

He comes!

What a quiet, empty place this is!

Patrash Pasha will be pleased!

Salaam Aleikum, most noble Sheik: the prisoner comes!

Bring him before me!

Aha! So it is you! It is you who tried to poison the servants of Patrash Pasha, infidel dog!

You mind your language!

We can do without the worthless clutter of your so-called civilisation!

What is your name?

My name? It won't mean a thing to you . . .

. . . but at home they call me Tintin.

Tintin! Can it be true? . . . Allah be praised . . . Come to my arms!

?

For years I have read of your exploits . . . Allah is good . . . that he should bring you to my humble tent!

A whole sequence to reshoot, thanks to you!

He's absolutely ruined my entrance!

Oh heavens. I've barged in on a film company!

You deserve to be . . .

I'm sorry . . . How could I know   . . . ?

What's going on here?

Sir Galahad here has wrecked my scene!

By Lucifer! Unless I'm much mistaken, you're the young man I had that little tiff with aboard the 'Isis'.

Why, it's Mr Rastapopoulos!

I'm sorry I lost my temper!

And I'm sorry if I messed up your film.

Pah! Think nothing of it! We're making a Superscope-Magnavista feature of "Arabian Knights". We've built a whole city not far from here.

I know. I saw it.

But what are you doing here, all by yourself in the middle of the desert? Come and explain . . .

Certainly . . .

An hour later . . .

. . . So there you are, Mr Rastapopoulos. That's my story. Remarkable, isn't it?

Indeed, dear boy. I find it fascinating!

I'm sorry we cannot keep you here, my friend.

You're very kind, but the captain of the dhow will be wondering where I am.

There she is, Snowy. We'll soon be back on board now.

Meanwhile . . .

Hmm . . . fresh instructions. We're to forget about Tintin, and look for gun-runners along the Arab coastline.

I can't see a soul on deck.

How odd, all gone . . . not so much as a whisker . . .

Sorry, I was wrong. At least puss stayed behind . . . Here, Snowy!

Wooah! Wooah!

Snowy, come here at once!

?

Great snakes! Machine-guns, under an old tarpaulin!

And rifles hidden beneath a layer of umbrellas!

I wonder where that cat went to . . .

. . . All these crates are packed with ammunition! It's like an arsenal down here!

More automatic weapons! What a fool I've been. It didn't cross my mind . . . this innocent little ship: gun-running!

Interesting, eh?

?

!

Saved!

Lucky for us he hooked himself . . .

Hurry up or he'll drown!

You'd better catch that animal while I take care of his master!

Stop, in the name of the law!

It's going to take more than that to catch me!

You're under arrest!

Help! Everybody out!

?

Help! He's dropped a grenade! We're going up!

Funny, something must have frightened him . . .

DANGER

EXP

EXP

EXP

Panic stations! . . . Cut the cables! . . . We're blowing up!

Goodness gracious! . . . Tintin!

Oh dear, we forgot!

What's up with them? One minute they arrest me, the next they bolt like a couple of rabbits.

A pity about Tintin . . .

Yes . . . I say, does a grenade take long to explode?

Lucky for us they ship grenades without explosive . . . otherwise we'd be sitting on a cloud by now, Snowy.

The fuse just went "phut".

TOP

Come on, Snowy, don't let's hang around here.

We'll head for the Cosmos camp. I'm sure Mr Rastapopoulos will be able to help us on our way.

There's the camp. I wonder what he will say when I tell him about our latest adventure.

My dear chap, it's exactly like a film. Anyone would think there was a plot to get rid of you!

Next morning . . .

Good luck!

Goodbye! . . . And thank you again!

Still no explosion . . .

Don't be impatient . . . Must be delayed action . . .

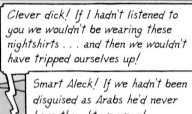

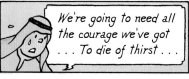

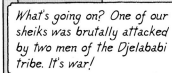

RECRUITING OFFICE

Tough nut, sir! ... Fancies himself! Refused to enlist!

A tough nut, eh? We'll see. You must educate him, corporal!

Left ... right ... left ... right ... pick 'em up there, you horrible layabouts!

Halt! Order arms! Enough for today. Forty miles route march tomorrow. Squad, dismiss!

A rest at last!

ALI-BHAI!

ALI-BHAI!

Some poor chap in trouble ...

You! Jump to it when I call you! Don't fool with me!

Who, me? I ...

Four days confined to barracks! Now, clean up the colonel's office ... And watch your step!

?

Stupid idiot! How could I forget I gave the name Ali-Bhai when I enlisted?

?

FLOR FINA

Great snakes! The cigars of the Pharaoh! With the identical band! It's incredible!

Maybe I can find a whole box of them ...

Got one! Hooray!

A spy! Call out the guard!

COLONEL FUAD COMMANDING OFFICER

Get moving, you men! Arrest him! Lock him up!

COLONEL COMM OFFIC

That's my luck! Just when I was getting to the bottom of the mystery . . .

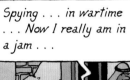

Spying . . . in wartime . . . Now I really am in a jam . . .

. . . The sentence of the court is that Private Ali-Bhai be shot at dawn . . . The execution will take place tomorrow . . . The sentence will be communicated to the prisoner forthwith!

Shot! . . . I'm going to be shot . . . My poor, poor Snowy . . . This is the end!

A note . . . "Have courage: help is at hand. A friend." A friend? . . . Here? . . .

My last night on earth. Unless . . .

Tintin! . . . Tintin! . . .

?

Who . . . who are you?

Ssh! . . . Here's a file. Cut through the bars.

Hurry up! It's nearly dawn . . .

RRRZ
RRRZ
RRRZ

Done it!

Come, quick!

No time to lose!

Coming!

Free!

HALT! . . . OR I FIRE!

!

27

A plane! . . . If I could only . . . No, there's a guard . . .

It's my only chance . . . I must try . . . Help! . . . Help!

Help! Help! Save me! The dog . . . It's gone mad . . . Stop it! . . .

Who? . . . Me?

It worked! He's bolted! We're free!

?

Whew! . . . We just got away in time!

What? He escaped? In an aeroplane, you say? Good-for-nothing-goatherds! Get fighters after him and shoot him down! You hear me?!

There . . . that speck on the horizon . . .

Fine . . . and he doesn't suspect we're on his tail . . .

Our lucky day, Snowy!

! RATATATATAT

Crumbs! Only one thing to do: dive!

RATATATATAT

Hooray! I've hit him!

That's what's known as a clean kill!

Mission accomplished, sir. We shot him down.

Good, well done!

Any more to come?

Now, I wonder where we are. Somewhere in India, I'm sure, but impossible to tell exactly.

!

Don't be afraid, old chap. Snowy wouldn't hurt a fly.

Wooah! Wooah!

Good heavens, you're ill. You're running a temperature . . . Wait, I've just the thing for you.

What he needs is a good dose of quinine . . .

A whole tube. That should be enough.

There, swallow that.

A lightning cure!

Hey! Take it easy, old man!

Put me down . . . at once!

Where in the world is he taking me?

?

Look, brother elephants, this young human has cured my fever.

They seem to be having a conference. Now I can slip away.

Hrrrrm! Hrrrrm! Stop, little human. You must stay with us . . . You are our elephant doctor.

Some days later . . .

You see, Snowy, when the elephants talk to one another they make a sort of trumpeting sound. I've been listening to them . . .

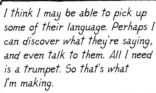

I think I may be able to pick up some of their language. Perhaps I can discover what they're saying, and even talk to them. All I need is a trumpet. So that's what I'm making.

It isn't all that difficult. SOL-LAH-TE-DOH means 'yes'. DOH-TE-LAH-SOL means 'no'. 'I want a drink' goes SOL-SOL-FAH-FAH . . . Of course the main problem is to get a good accent.

Phew! I'm hot! . . . I wonder . . . Why don't I try . . .

♪♩♩♩♪♪

Did he understand?

He did! He's coming back! Hooray, I've learnt to talk Elephant!

Now you stay here. I'm going for a walk.

It's time I did a bit of exploring.

!

Kih-Oskh! The symbol, here! . . . It's unbelievable!!

35

Who on earth could have painted that sign?

The ♪ sheik ♩ of ♪ Araby ♫

It can't be!

Doctor Sarcophagus!

Doctor! Hello! How in the world did you get here?

Tell me what happened . . . everything, since you floated away in the coffin . . .

Ssh! Not so loud!

I'll tell you. But you must promise to keep it a secret.

Of course . . . Now then . . .

Well, absolutely between ourselves, I'm the Pharaoh Rameses II!

Tweet, tweet! . . . Don't tell a soul . . . Nobody knows . . . I'm travelling incognito.

Poor Doctor Sarcophagus . . . He's completely mad. I shan't get anything out of him until he's cured. But where can I find a doctor?

Where? . . . Of course! That's easy!

I used to play the piano too when I was a boy . . .

A little later . . .

That's the whole story, doctor. Do you think the poor fellow might be cured one day?

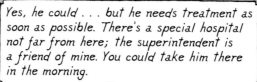

Yes, he could . . . but he needs treatment as soon as possible. There's a special hospital not far from here; the superintendent is a friend of mine. You could take him there in the morning.

Meanwhile, you're my guest. I've just fixed a small party for tonight: do join us.

Later . . .

Tintin . . . Our good padre the Reverend Peacock . . .

. . . Mr and Mrs Snowball . . .

. . . the well-known poet, Zloty.

That's a strange weapon you have there. Isn't it a Hindu dagger?

Yes, a kukri . . .

It's made of steel . . . a deadly little toy! . . . I was given it by a fakir. He told me it had magic powers . . . It's supposed to point to anyone whose life is in danger.

I'll get it down for you to see . . .

!

OH!!!

I'm so sorry. I do hope you won't take it as a bad omen.

Please don't worry. It's just a coincidence . . . Anyway, I'm not scared of omens!

BANG

Don't be alarmed, it's only the wind. I think we're in for a storm.

AAAAAAH

Quick! . . . Upstairs! . . . That sounded like Doctor Sarcophagus.

Empty!! He must have gone out of the window.

HELP! . . . SAVE ME!

My wife! . . . That's my wife!

OOH!

She fainted just as I came in . . .

No one!

Oh! . . . Oh! . . . It was horrible . . . A ghost . . . I saw a ghost!

The dagger has gone! . . . Look! It was here on the table . . .

Oh, Sahib! Sahib! . . . The spirits have come for us! I saw one . . . all in white . . . running into the jungle!

First time I've heard of a spirit nipping off with a dagger! . . . Anyway, no good chasing him tonight. We'll search in the morning.

Next morning...

The young sahib went out at dawn, into the forest.

Try not to lose the trail, Snowy...

Look!... There's his hat!

Yes, it's certainly his. We're on the right track... He's somewhere around...

What do you think of that, Snowy? Smart, eh?

!

Help! He's gone berserk!... Run for it!

Lucky his arm got tangled in the creeper. Otherwise...

?

So! You cannot resist me!

Ooh, pretty little peashooter!

BANG

Whoopee! What a jolly game! Ram-Ram's playing bang-bang!

I'll shoot you, naughty thing!

BANG

BANG

Whew! Thank goodness! . . . Just a butterfly.

Bang-bang all gone.

Never mind, let's go.

The fakir managed to escape . . . No use going after him . . . Let's concentrate on the poet . . . He can only mean that Zloty fellow.

A few minutes later . . .

Let's have the cards on the table, Mr Zloty. Someone's trying to murder me. And you're going to tell me precisely what you know about it . . .

Me? . . . But I don't understand . . .

You're lying! Talk, and talk fast!

Or else . . . bang!

Wait! . . . I . . . yes . . . I . . .

I don't know very much . . . There's an international gang of drug-smugglers . . . They're determined to get rid of you . . .

And you're a member of the gang?

Yes . . . No . . . I mean . . . There is a branch of the organisation here . . . You were recognised and someone reported to the boss . . .

And who is the boss?

Just a minute . . . The boss was furious that you were still alive: he gave orders for you to be liquidated . . . Sarcophagus was to do it, while he was hypnotised . . .

But the boss . . . Tell me his name!

No . . . I can't . . . it's impossible . . . They are merciless to traitors . . . it's horrible . . .

You're going to tell me, now!

I . . . he . . . his name is . . .

!

Someone was hiding outside the shutters . . .

Too late . . . I'm done for . . . It's their revenge . . . This arrow is poisoned with Rajaijah juice, the poison of madness.

The boss . . . film . . . don't trust . . .

Quick! Quick!

Here we come ♪♪ gathering ♪♪ nuts in May . . .

Come along, children, playtime is over now . . .

Who can tell me who succeeded Rameses II?

Me, sir . . . Napoleon.

Later . . .

Now we've got two madmen on our hands.

We'll send them to hospital tomorrow.

Next morning . . .

Here's a letter for the superintendent.

Ha! ha! Off to hospital, my clever friend. With that letter they'll certainly give you a warm welcome!

Here's a letter from Dr Finney about these two patients.

Hmm . . . Yes . . . I see . . . Quite so . . .

Orderly, look after these gentlemen, please.

Will you come with me? . . . Just a few formalities . . .

Certainly.

There's nothing to be afraid of. They're quite harmless.

This is the sort of ward we shall use for treating your poor friends.

SLAM

?

"He will give you this letter himself. He will tell you it concerns his two companions . . ."

". . . He is extremely dangerous. You should trick him into entering a cell, rather than force him. He will keep on insisting that he is absolutely sane . . ."

So, gentlemen, your unhappy friend will have all possible care.

We have complete confidence in you.

Goodbye, gentlemen.

Happy birthday, nanny!

Hello . . . yes boss. I copied the doctor's writing, and substituted another letter . . . It made out that Tintin himself was mad, not the others, and . . .

WOOAH! WOOAH!

THUMP THUMP THUMP

THUMP THUMP THUMP

If you don't keep quiet we'll put you in a strait-jacket! Understand?

If this is some sort of game, doctor, it's time it stopped. It isn't me that's mad, it's the other two I brought here . . .

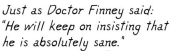

Just as Doctor Finney said: "He will keep on insisting that he is absolutely sane."

Mad? They think I'm mad? It's unbelievable!

Here is your soup.

My soup?

Are you joking?

That's what I think of your soup!

?

Ye-o-o-ow! . . . Ye-o-o-w!

This is it! Now or never . . .

Help! Help!

Just the wall, and I'm free!

Crikey! How can I get over that?!

?

Oh no! My escape . . . cut off!

I'll have to jump for it: if I stop I'm done for! Here goes . . .

Hey, wait for me!

Confound it! He's escaped!

Wooah! Wooah!

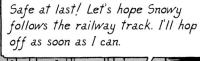

Safe at last! Let's hope Snowy follows the railway track. I'll hop off as soon as I can.

!

Well, well, what a surprise to see your face again! We'd lost you completely!

To be precise: we'd completely lost face!

Tintin! Now I shall never see him again . . .

? ? ?

I've got him!

Me too!

Goodness gracious! It's the ticket collector!

To be precise: we've collected a ticket!

He can't have gone too far.

No, we aren't too far gone.

Hello? Jamjah . . . the station? One of our patients has escaped, jumped aboard a train heading in your direction. I'll describe him for you . . .

The train is stopping.

Someone must have pulled the communication cord.

Yes, quite a young man . . . He asked me to hide him, so I pulled the alarm. But as soon as the train stopped he ran off. He went that way . . .

SETHRU-JAMJAH

He can't have much start: we'll soon catch up with him.

Have a good time!

SETHRU-JAMJAH

This track goes on for ever. Where does it end?

Good! Someone to ask.

Excuse me, madam, I'm sorry to intrude, but can you tell me when the last train went by?

Miserable dog! Do you not know that I am a sacred cow?

You?! A sacred cow? A likely story!

You think so?! I'll teach you to mind your manners, vulgar little cur!

Where's the mongrel gone?

MOO-OW!...

Wooah! Wooah!

Sacrilege! . . . A dog is attacking our sacred cow!

Kill it!

Sacrilege! Kill it! Kill it!

We will slay it on the altar of Siva!

An hour later . . .

How can I get off the platform without a ticket? . . .

No mistake, it's him all right . . . Matches the description exactly . . .

What do they want with me?

Crumbs! Now I understand . . . My escape has been reported . . .

Hey, you! Stop!

STOP! . . .

Lucky for me I bought some bananas!

One . . .

INDIAN RAILWAYS

Two . . .

Just wait, clever-dick . . . We'll pay you back!

WAY OUT

And that's for number three . . .

ZZIP

All that, just to end up in a strait-jacket. Poor Snowy, if you could see your master now!

Meanwhile . . .

O Siva-the-destroyer, graciously accept the sacrifice I am about to offer.

The superintendent will be pleased to recover . . .

. . . this awkward customer!

. . . The patient! Where's he gone?

Quick! Look around! He can't be far away.

Free! . . . I'm free! . . .

Meanwhile . . .

Die, infidel dog!

Stay your hand, servant of Siva! The god will not accept so mean a sacrifice!

He's gone: it's all clear.

To be precise: the all clear's gone!

Quick . . . untie him.

How wrong I was. They're really pretty good chaps!

Ha ha! If we follow the dog we'll find the master.

And in the jungle . . .

By the holy brahmin! Look, Highness, look!

See! We are catching young man in tiger-trap!

I'm sorry to trouble you, but I wonder if you'd mind . . .

But of course!

It is fortunate that we happened to pass this way.

How can I thank you enough, Mr . . . Mr . . . ?

. . . The Maharaja of Gaipajama. How do you do.

Highness! Highness! See! On the branch! The lord of the jungle!

BANG

Great gods! I missed it!

GRRR GRRR GRRR

Your tiger, Highness!

?

We will return to the palace. You are my guest, Mr . . . Mr . . . ?

Tintin, reporter.

And that evening . . .

?

By Siva! . . . That music!

No one! No one at all . . . Not a sign . . .

It's horrible . . . I must tell you . . . My father and my brother both went mad, one after the other. Each time, just before they became ill, the same unearthly music was heard outside the palace . . .

This time I am sure it is for me . . . It is a warning . . .

. . . Rajaijah, the poison of madness . . .

Maharaja, when your father and your brother went mad, was there any sign of a wound, a puncture, on the neck or arm?

No, nothing . . . why?

Were they perhaps trying to fight the traffic in narcotics? Opium, for instance?

Indeed they were. And I am continuing their struggle. The poppy from which opium is made flourishes in this region. The drug traffickers terrorise my people. They force the peasants to grow poppies instead of food, and purchase . . .

. . . the crop for a miserable sum. Then, when the unhappy people need the rice they should have grown for themselves, they have to buy it from the smugglers at exorbitant prices. I never stop fighting the devilish organisation.

Good. We will work together. Listen carefully, Highness . . .

That night . . .

You see? . . . There . . . That window in the middle . . .

Magic rope, obey your master!

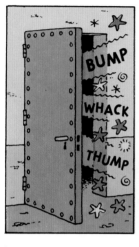

THWACK

Not a bad day's work! . . . I must say I was lucky to be called first . . . Now, let's have a look at the faces of our jungle Ku Klux Klan!

The fakir, a Japanese, Mr and Mrs Snowball, the colonel who sentenced me to death, and the Maharaja's secretary . . . It's fantastic!

?

Tintin! . . . Him!! . . . Here!!!

What a cheek, thinking he could tie me up . . . Me, a fully qualified fakir!

The fakir! He's escaped!

CLACK

Great snakes! I mustn't let him get away!

BANG

Aha! Now I really have you in my power!

Gangsters! A good thing I wasn't fooled!

Impossible to get him. You keep him occupied while I make a break with the kid.

Now where is he? I can't see . . .

Hands up, Houdini! And drop your gun!

?

There, that's better. Just a minor detail, but my gun wasn't loaded.

What a coincidence! My gun happens to be empty too. So it's just the two of us . . .

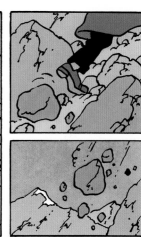

!

I couldn't have done it better myself!

While Snowy guards the fakir, I'll go after the mystery man . . .

Diavolo! Can I never be rid of him? . . . But wait . . .

Come along, dear boy, just a little bit nearer . . .

HELP!!

... Missed! But I'm not finished yet . . .

!!!

CRACK

?

Poor wretch. Who was he? . . . I wonder if we shall ever know . . . or has he taken his secret with him?

Ah, there's the prince. I must get him back to the palace.

A little later . . .

My son!

Daddy!

Now, if your Highness will excuse me, I must say goodbye and start on my long journey home.

No, no, Tintin, I don't want you to go!

Allow me to insist, Tintin. You must stay for a few days at least.

Thank you, your Highness. I shall be delighted.

Hip hip hooray!

IOS KING NISHES

AIRO, Monday ion grows here e fate of millionaire agnate Rasta- s, reported missing ay from his desert mp. No news has ceived since his un- ed departure in his e plane for an un- n destination. Search s have been operating dawn in desert areas e west.

OON SHOT

DRUG GANG SMASHE

ROYAL HOSTAGE FREED

Reporter Tintin cracked the final link in an inter- national drug-smuggling chain, and following a dramatic mountain chase the boy Crown Prince of Gaipajama, held hostage by the gang leader, was freed. The narcotics boss, whose identity is still a mystery, plunged to his death down a precipice. has not yet been

An informal shot of Messrs. Thomson and Thom son, detectives in the drug case, answering an urge call to headquarters.

A few days later . . .

Long live Rameses II!

Play up! Play up! Now! Pass to the wing!

! !

Hooray for Tutankhamen!

A goal! A goal! . . . Magnificent shot!

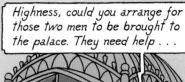

Highness, could you arrange for those two men to be brought to the palace. They need help . . .

And later that day . . .

Greetings, most noble Pharaoh!

They're still quite mad . . .

Bring cigars and a drink for our guests.

Stop! Remember, it is forbidden to touch the cigars of the Pharaoh!

?

Tell me quickly, where did you find these cigars?

They belonged to the Maharaja's former secretary. I knew he kept these hidden away. So when I couldn't find any of our usual brand, I brought these.

Just as I thought . . . The identical cigars! We found them in the tomb of Kih-Oskh . . . And the Arab colonel had some. Now let me see . . .

As I expected, they're fakes. The band, an outer covering of tobacco, and inside, opium! Quite a simple trick, but it fooled the police of half the world.

Well done, Tintin! . . . But what about our friends here?

The Rolls? Thank you, my man.

The gentlemen's conveyance is waiting.

They will be well cared for . . . And you, my young friend, have earned a good holiday. Maybe a nice quiet cruise . . . now that we have seen the last of that evil gang.

I hope you are right, Highness, I certainly hope so . . . But somehow, I wonder . . .

HERGÉ.

THE END